This Ladybird Book belongs to:

_____

_____

_____

_____

This Ladybird retelling
by
Molly Perham

Ladybird books are widely available, but in case of
difficulty may be ordered by post or telephone from:

Ladybird Books – Cash Sales Department
Littlegate Road Paignton Devon TQ3 3BE
Telephone 01803 554761

A catalogue record for this book is available
from the British Library

Published by Ladybird Books Ltd Loughborough Leicestershire UK
Ladybird Books Inc Auburn Maine 04210 USA

FAVOURITE TALES

The Princess and the Frog

illustrated
by
SUE KING

based on a traditional folk tale

Once upon a time there was a king who had seven daughters. All of them were charming but the youngest princess was even more delightful than the rest.

As she played in the palace garden with her favourite golden ball, it seemed as though the sun shone more brightly and the birds sang more sweetly to see her there.

One hot day, the Princess went into the forest and sat down beside a pool. She started to toss her golden ball up into the air and catch it.

She threw the ball higher and higher into the air until… *SPLASH!* the ball fell into the pool and sank down into the deep water.

The Princess was so upset that she began to sob.

"Why are you crying, Princess?" croaked a voice nearby.

The tearful Princess looked up in surprise and saw a frog sitting at the edge of the pool.

"My ball has fallen into the water!" she sobbed. "It is lost for ever."

"Perhaps I can help," said the frog. "What will you give me if I find your ball?"

"Anything you like," cried the Princess. "My dresses, my jewels, or even my golden crown."

"I don't want any of those," said the frog. "All I want is for you to love me and be my friend. I want to eat from your plate and sleep in your bed."

"You can have anything you want if you find my ball, I promise," said the Princess eagerly, certain that the frog could never live like a human.

SPLOSH! The frog dived into the pool and disappeared beneath the water.

"He will never find it," thought the Princess.

But in a minute the frog's head appeared above the water with the golden ball.

The Princess was so happy to have her favourite toy again that she forgot her promise immediately. She picked up the golden ball and ran off through the forest to her father's castle.

"Wait for me! Wait for me!" cried the frog, jumping along as fast as he could. But he couldn't catch up with the Princess.

Next day, as the Princess sat at the dinner table with the King and her sisters, there came a knock at the door, followed by a croaking sound.

At first the Princess pretended not to hear. She was dreadfully afraid that she recognised the sound outside.

"Princess! Princess! Let me come in!" came the croaking again. The Princess got up crossly and opened the door.

The frog who had helped her the previous day hopped into the room. But before he could speak, the Princess rudely pushed him out and slammed the door.

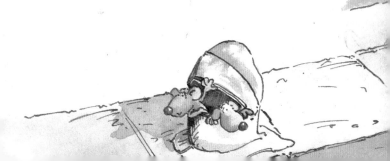

The King saw that his youngest
daughter had turned pale.

"What has frightened you, my dear?"
he asked. "Is there a giant outside the
door who has come to take you away?"

"No, Father," the Princess replied.
"It's only a horrible, slimy frog. He
rescued my ball from the pool and in
return I promised that he could eat
from my plate and sleep in my bed."

"Then you must keep your promise," said the King sternly. "Open the door!"

So the Princess reluctantly opened the door and the frog hopped in.

"Lift me onto the table," he said, "so that I can eat from your plate."

The Princess shuddered at the idea of touching the slimy frog, but her father was watching her. She picked up the frog and watched him feed from her plate, hardly able to eat a bite herself.

At the end of the meal, the frog said, "I am very tired. Please take me to your room so that I can share your soft bed."

The Princess burst into tears, but the King said, "The frog helped you and now you must help him. Pick him up and take him to your room."

When she reached her bedroom, the Princess put the frog down in the farthest corner. But the frog said, "Lift me up and put me on your bed, or I will tell your father."

So the Princess picked up the frog and dropped him quickly onto her silken pillow.

Suddenly, before her very eyes, the frog turned into a handsome prince.

"Please don't be frightened," he said.

The Prince told her how he had been turned into a frog by an evil witch.

"Only a princess could break the spell by taking me to live with her," he explained. "Now, thanks to you, I am free at last."

The Prince had watched the Princess playing in the forest and had fallen in love with her. "Do you think you could love me and be my friend now?" he asked. The Princess was so happy that she could hardly speak.

The Prince and the Princess were married and lived happily ever after.